WILD THING

LAWRENCE HIGH YEARBOOK SERIES
BOOK I

WILD THING

DAVID A. POULSEN

KEY PORTER BOOKS

Library and Archives Canada Cataloguing in Publication

Poulsen, David A., 1946–
Wild thing / David A. Poulsen. (Lawrence High yearbook)

ISBN-13: 978-1-55263-931-3, ISBN-10: 1-55263-931-2

I. Title. II. Series: Poulsen, David A., 1946 – . Lawrence High yearbook series.

PS8581.O848W54 2007   jC813'.54   C2007-901960-9

The publisher gratefully acknowledges the support of the Canada Council for the Arts and the Ontario Arts Council for its publishing program. We acknowledge the support of the Government of Ontario through the Ontario Media Development Corporation's Ontario Book Initiative.

We acknowledge the financial support of the Government of Canada through the Book Publishing Industry Development Program (BPIDP) for our publishing activities.

Key Porter Books Limited
Six Adelaide Street East, Tenth Floor
Toronto, Ontario
Canada M5C 1H6
www.keyporter.com

Text design and formatting: Marijke Friesen

Printed and bound in Canada

07 08 09 10 11 5 4 3 2 1

To the real Mr. White and all the teachers like him.
Especially the ones who taught me.
I didn't appreciate you then but I sure do now.

1

The guy was in the wrong school. That was obvious. Nobody who looked like that, with the weird hair and the hippie clothes—even sandals—nobody like that belonged at Lawrence High.

See, Lawrence is a sports school. They call us the "jock joint" at other schools. Which is fine with us. We figure they're just jealous.

And football is the sport, ever since K.Y. Briggs came to Lawrence. That's right, K.Y. Briggs—nine years with the Denver Broncos, two seasons with over a thousand yards rushing, three years in the Canadian Football League over in

Saskatchewan—the guy is a future Hall of Famer. And he's our coach.

The Lawrence Cowboys haven't had a losing season since K.Y. Briggs took over the team. That was five seasons ago. We even went to the City finals twice, but our school lost both times to St. Joseph's. Not this year though. This year we're gonna do it to those St. Joe's creeps. And then it's on to Regionals.

My name is Marcel Boileau, but everybody calls me French, because I was born in Quebec. I'm a halfback. A starter too. Not bad for a tenth-grade rookie.

My best friend, Denny Hillman, and I are the only tenth-grade starters on the team. Denny's big enough to impersonate a barn. That's why he's on the "O" line. "O" stands for offensive, if you don't know football.

Anyway, I was standing in the hall outside our homeroom with Denny when we first saw the new kid—the one with the sandals. He was coming right toward us.

"Geez, check out the dork!" Denny practically yelled it, then he made these gross noises like a balloon makes when you let the air out of it.

I didn't say anything, but I have to admit, I stared pretty hard at the guy. I couldn't help it. I mean, you don't have to actually play a sport to fit in at Lawrence. But it helps if you can at least like tell the difference between football and ... say, table tennis. This guy didn't look like he knew the difference.

He was passing right in front of us.

"Ooh-whee!" Denny made a noise like he was calling hogs. Denny's pretty good with noises. "Check it out. What we have here is a gen-you-whine, hippie-dippy scuzball."

The guy stopped and looked at Denny. His eyes came up to Denny's chin. No higher, for sure. I figured he'd back off when he realized how big Denny actually was. But he didn't. Didn't even flinch. All he did, in this voice that was soft and low and blizzard cold, was say, "Suck an egg, Meat."

For a second I thought Denny was going to drill the guy. I mean, I've known Denny since grade school, and nobody has ever called him anything but Denny. That's because ever since he was eight years old he's been a head taller and forty pounds heavier than the next biggest kid.

For a long time, the next biggest kid was Lois Mead. In fact, if Lois were still around, she could probably play on the "O" line at Lawrence. But she moved to the coast a couple of years ago.

Anyway, the guy with the hair and the sandals calls Denny "Meat" and then walks away like they'd been talking about the weather or something. I figured he was either a very brave guy or a terrific actor.

Denny was so shocked he didn't do anything, or even say anything. Just stood there with a totally stunned look on that big face of his.

I don't want you to get the idea that Denny is a bully or anything. He's not. In fact, I don't remember ever seeing him in a real fight. Maybe when you're that big, you don't have to fight. All the same, I don't like to get on the wrong side of Denny.

Just then, he grabbed me by the shoulder, which reminded me why I don't like to be on his bad side.

"He's history." His voice was sort of like a growl. "That guy is history, French."

Denny probably would've headed off down the hall after the guy right then if Pam Parlee hadn't come along at that exact moment. There's one thing I've never been able to figure. How does a guy who's big enough to bench press buses turn into a soggy bowl of corn flakes when a certain girl shows up?

Denny had been trying to work up the courage to ask Pam out for about two years, but so far no luck. I'd been there a few times when he tried; it was pretty pathetic. The words that came out of Denny's mouth were like some foreign language. None of them sounded anything like "Do you want to go out with me?" So, no date so far.

"Hi, Denny. Hi, French." Pam is one of those people who always seems to be in a good mood.

"Hi, Pam." Denny smiled and let go of my shoulder. Finally. I nodded hi to Pam.

"How do you think you did on the chem exam?" she asked Denny.

"OK, I guess."

That was probably pushing the truth a little. I might not be great in chemistry but Denny is close to a disaster.

"That's good." Pam smiled a cute, freckly smile. "If you feel like studying together sometime, let me know. You could come over to my place and we could make popcorn or something."

I was sure Denny was going to faint. Which is a scary idea. When people that size fall down, they can do serious damage to smaller people standing next to them.

"Yeah...sure..." Denny was starting to stutter. I figured he was going to break into the foreign language thing any second.

"Did you guys see our newest student?" Pam sounded excited.

"Yeah," I said. Denny just nodded.

"Isn't he gorgeous?" Pam gushed. "I heard he's in a band. His stage name is Wild Thing!"

"Wow," Denny said in a voice that didn't have much wow in it.

"Well, gotta go." Pam tossed her hair and started off down the hall. "See ya, French. Don't forget to call me if you want to study together, Denny."

We stood there and watched her go. "Awright!" I looked at Denny. "Popcorn and Pam. Sweet. Perfect, in fact. I bet you could learn to love chemistry."

"Yeah," Denny said with a shrug, "but can you believe that Wild Thing stuff? And she likes the guy. That settles it. He's toast."

From the way Denny fired the door open on the way into class, I was real glad I wasn't the Wild Thing.

2

Denny was still mad after school. I could tell by the way he was hitting the sled at football practice.

The sled is this thing on runners that guys practice their blocking against. Usually it takes two strong guys to move it even a little. Denny hit it so hard, Coach Briggs had to jump out of the way to keep from being run over.

I figured if Denny was still upset at Wild Thing when we played St. Joseph's, he could destroy their entire "D" line. Which, come to think of it, would be okay.

Practice was going along more or less like normal. Grunts, groans, some guys laughing, some limping around. Near the end, there was a drill where the "O" line and "D" line guys were throwing balls back and forth.

A lot of the time the big guys don't ever touch the ball in games. But Coach Briggs wants to make sure everybody knows what to do if there's a chance to recover a fumble or intercept a pass. Coach is really thorough about stuff like that.

So there they were tossing the ball back and forth. I was taking a few hand-offs from our quarterback, Carter Kent. That's when I saw it... him. There was ol' Wild Thing himself, standing on the sidelines watching the practice.

I looked over and saw that Denny was also aware that Lawrence's newest student was watching us.

Now, Denny might be strong and everything, but one thing he doesn't do real well is catch a football. Especially if he's not paying total attention, which he wasn't, since he was busy watching Wild Thing watch us.

So naturally the very next time the ball came Denny's way, he dropped it. And that's when I decided Wild Thing must have a death wish. Because when Denny dropped the ball, Wild Thing yelled, "Nice catch, Meat!"

I could see that Denny wanted to go over there and squish the guy down into one of his sandals but of course he couldn't. Not if he didn't want Coach Briggs all over his case. Which nobody wants, not even Denny.

So instead he picked up the ball and fired it straight at Wild Thing. Denny might not be able to catch a football but he sure can throw one. Hard. And that was about the hardest throw I ever saw him make.

Most of the guys were watching. It's a good thing, because if I'd been the only one, everybody would've called me a liar when I told them what happened.

Wild Thing, who was carrying books in one hand, reached up with the other hand and caught the ball—a ball that was travelling at pretty close to light speed!

It was like...unbelievable! Catching a football with one hand is not all that easy. Sometimes at practice the backs and receivers fool around and try to make these spectacular one-handed grabs. We drop the ball about ninety-nine percent of the time. And believe me, that ball isn't going nearly as fast as the one Denny threw. And we're not holding books in our other hand.

After he'd caught it, Wild Thing flipped the ball back to Denny, who dropped it again.

"Maybe you should try Velcro, Meat." Wild Thing laughed this crazy laugh.

After practice I caught up with Denny. "Did you see him catch that thing?"

"Yeah, I saw. He couldn't do it again if he had to."

"Maybe not," I said, "but he looks like he knows what to do with a football."

"Don't matter, I'm still gonna kill the—" Denny stopped talking and stopped walking at the same time. I stopped too. Right in front of us Coach Briggs was having a conversation with Wild Thing.

"What's Coach talking to that idiot for?"

Denny stood there banging his helmet against his leg.

"I don't know."

We had just started walking again when Coach Briggs turned and called, "Hey Hillman, come over here for a minute. You too, French."

We looked at each other and walked over to where Coach Briggs and Wild Thing were standing. Coach Briggs was smiling, something he didn't do that often.

"I want you guys to meet W.T. Zahara," Coach Briggs said. "He's a new student here at Lawrence."

Denny looked grizzly bear grumpy. "We've met," he mumbled.

"Yeah," I said.

"Well, that's great then," Coach Briggs was still smiling, "because I've just invited W.T. here to try out for the squad. Turns out he played two years in Vancouver."

Denny and I looked at each other again but we didn't say anything.

Coach Briggs slapped Denny on the shoulder pads. "And I've decided to appoint you to be his team buddy. You know, show him around, help him get settled in."

"Me?" Denny's voice had a squeak in it.

"Sure," Coach Briggs's smile had become a grin. "I know you'll do a great job."

The coach walked away then leaving us standing there—Denny, bigger than ever in his football equipment, Wild Thing in his sandals, and me with my mouth open.

I could tell Denny wasn't happy but you didn't argue with Coach Briggs. "Well...uh...I guess you might as well come into the dressing room and ... uh ... meet the guys," Denny said without looking at Wild Thing.

"Nope," Wild Thing shook his head. "Got a band rehearsal. I'll be at practice tomorrow. You can start being my buddy then...Meat."

He turned and wandered off and Denny started after him. I grabbed him by the arm.

"Don't do it," I said. "You start something with him and you'll get cut from the team for sure."

"Yeah," Denny said slowly, "but what did the

coach ask him out for anyway? The guy's a loser."

"He doesn't catch like a loser," I reminded him.

Denny ignored me. "Maybe Briggs likes guys who have initials for names. Yeah, that's it...K.Y. and W.T....maybe they're both some kind of... weirdos."

I knew Denny didn't mean that. "I doubt it." I shook my head. "Besides, W.T. aren't his real initials."

"Huh?"

"W.T.—Wild Thing. Get it?"

"Oh...yeah...yeah, I knew that."

We walked into the locker room. As soon as we got inside the door, we both knew something was wrong.

Football locker rooms are crazy places most of the time. Guys are flicking towels or telling jokes. The tunes are playing real loud. But this time when we walked in, it was totally quiet. Like it is at halftime if Coach Briggs is giving us crap for playing bad.

Carter Kent looked up at us. "Better check your stuff, you guys. We've been robbed."

"What?" Denny and I both said it at the same time.

"Somebody was in here when we were on the field and cleaned out most of our wallets."

Denny and I ran to our lockers. I didn't even have to look in mine. My wallet was lying on the floor. It was open.

"Man, I had twenty bucks. It's gone," I heard Denny say.

I looked in my wallet. "Yeah, they got me for twelve bucks, too. Even stole my ticket to the dance."

Denny came over and sat down next to me. "You know who did this, don't you?"

"Huh?"

"Who didn't want to come into the dressing room tonight? Who had a band rehearsal? Huh? Who?"

"You think...?"

"No, I don't think. I know. We've never had our locker room ripped off before. Suddenly they let some jerk into the school and our money's gone."

"Who are you talking about?" Carter Kent called from across the locker room.

Denny stood up and looked at me, then over at Carter. "I'm talking about Wild Thing!"

3

Next day at practice a lot of the guys wanted to do some serious damage to Wild Thing's body.

But Coach Briggs got wind of it and took Denny and me aside.

"If anything happens to W.T., I'll be holding you two personally responsible," he said.

Denny kicked the floor a couple of times. "Yeah, but—"

"No buts," Coach cut him off. "You heard me. Nobody knows for sure who ripped off the locker room and when we do find out, I'll be the one handing out the discipline. Got it?"

Denny didn't say anything.

"*Got it?*"

"Okay, Coach, I got it," Denny said. I nodded.

"Good, now let's have a good practice. We have to get ready for Central."

Denny and I put out the word to the guys that Coach didn't want any funny business. So, practice went off pretty normally.

I didn't notice our new player much until near the end of practice. We were doing a one-on-one blocking drill, which I hate because sometimes the little guys wind up going against the big guys. Which is usually painful for the little guys. Like me.

Sure enough, eventually Wild Thing and Denny squared off against one another. Wild Thing was supposed to block Denny and keep him away from an imaginary quarterback.

When Coach yelled "go," Denny let out this blood-curdling banshee scream and started toward Wild Thing. The big guy's arms were up and I knew he had it in his mind to tear the long-haired head right off ol' W.T.

Except when Denny got there, Wild Thing suddenly dropped down and stuck a shoulder into Denny's knees. Denny came down hard—so hard that I heard the air coming out of him from where I was.

I'll say one thing for Denny, though. Even though he must have been in big-time pain and probably couldn't breathe, he got up and walked away like nothing had happened.

"Nice block, W.T." Coach Briggs said.

A little later we were scrimmaging. Coach had Wild Thing playing wide receiver and he made some catches that even Denny couldn't believe. I was starting to think this guy could actually help our team.

We found out just how much he could help us in the game against Central. The Central Lions are a pretty good team, usually in the top three or four in the city. Coach Briggs warned us things could be a little tough. He was worried we might be looking ahead a couple weeks to the game with St. Joseph's and kind of overlook Central.

Right before the game, something weird happened. When the coach finished his pep talk he asked us if we had any questions, like he always does.

One of the guys, Billy Cameron, a linebacker, put up his hand and said, "Coach, I thought we had a hair rule on this team."

Right away, the whole place went quiet. Everybody knew who he was talking about. It was pretty obvious, with Wild Thing sitting on the other side of the locker room with about four inches of hair sticking out from under his helmet.

"So?" Coach asked.

"Well, what about him?" Billy pointed at Wild Thing.

"Yeah," Denny piped up. "How come he doesn't have to follow the rule?"

"W.T. talked to me about it and I made an exception in his case. His hair is part of his career image." Coach Briggs glared at the two of them. "Besides, five minutes before we go on the field isn't what I call a good time to discuss team rules."

That was it; no more was said. But it was the first time I'd ever seen what you could call a clubhouse revolt on our team. Sports reporters are always going on about that stuff in pro sports and how it can wreck a good team, but I never thought about it with the Cowboys. Not until that minute, that is.

We played like jerks in the first quarter, and we were lucky to be tied at halftime. It was 13–13. The coach didn't get on us all that bad during the break, which surprised me. Just before we went back on the field, I saw him take Carter Kent to one side and talk to him for a couple of minutes.

The first time we got the ball in the third quarter, Carter called for a long pass to Wild Thing. It was just like in practice. Wild Thing made this fingertip catch and outran the other team's safety like the guy was wearing lead shoes.

When it was over, we'd won 40–19 and Wild Thing had three touchdowns, all in the second half. In the locker room after the game, it was pretty quiet, considering we'd won.

Nobody really knew what to say to Wild Thing. So we didn't say anything. Nobody congratulated him, but nobody hassled him either. It was like he wasn't there. Sort of weird, really.

As we were walking out of the locker room Pam Parlee came running up.

"Great game, you guys!"

"Thanks," I said and Denny grinned like a dog getting its belly rubbed.

"Are you going to the dance tomorrow night?" Pam asked us.

"Yeah, I guess so," Denny nodded.

"I'll have to get another ticket," I said. "Mine was stolen when our dressing room got ripped off."

Just then Wild Thing walked by.

"Way to go, W.T. You were awesome," Pam told him.

"Thanks." Wild Thing smiled and kept walking.

"See you at the dance," Pam called.

Wild Thing turned and winked at Pam. "I'll be there."

"Did you hear?" Pam turned back to us. "Wild Thing's band The Heavy Breathers are going to be playing. Isn't that great?"

I looked over at Denny. The puppy dog grin was gone. I moved away before he decided to take it out on my shoulder again.

4

The dance was awesome. The Heavy Breathers were great and Wild Thing was excellent, I have to admit. He was the lead guitar player and he could make that thing talk, no kidding.

Speaking of talking, Pam Parlee and Denny were doing quite a bit of that. And dancing too. With each other, I mean.

I got in a few dances myself with a cute red-head in ninth grade. Annette Difolia's her name. Real pretty and real smart but she doesn't like football very much. Too bad. Other than that, she was almost perfect.

I threw in a few exotic moves on the dance floor. And Annette looked pretty good out there herself.

I was just starting to think maybe my brutal love life was turning around when suddenly she announced she had to go. Her mom was picking her up at 11:30. After that I didn't have much to do but watch Denny and Pam slow dance. Right up until the band took a break, that is.

Denny headed off to get drinks for Pam and him. When he got back you can guess who was standing real close to Pam, talking her up like crazy. Wild Thing was wearing this vest thing with no shirt and he was all sweaty. I guess girls must dig that kind of stuff because Pam was smiling a lot and talking like she was out of breath.

When Denny got back with the drinks, he parked himself between Wild Thing and Pam. I ambled over closer in case there was some action which, of course, I wouldn't have wanted to miss.

"I brought you a pop, Pam," Denny said.

"Thanks, Denny." Pam kept looking at Wild Thing even when she was talking to Denny.

"Didn't you bring me one?" Wild Thing had a big grin on his face.

"Get your own," Denny said.

"You're a real prince, Meat."

Denny turned around and stood face to face with Wild Thing. "I'm only going to tell you this once. Don't call me that again."

Pam put her hand on Denny's arm. "Hey you guys, lighten up, okay? Let's just have some fun tonight."

"Good idea." Wild Thing was still grinning. "But you'd have a lot more fun if you were with somebody else."

"Take a hike." Denny's face was getting redder.

"We're having a party at our drummer's place after," Wild Thing told Pam. "How about it? You wanna come?"

"Well...I don't know." I could see Pam was having a tough time making up her mind.

Wild Thing shrugged. "Look, I have to go play now, but let me know if you feel like coming along. See you later, Meat."

He started toward the stage, but Denny

caught hold of him and almost tore the vest right off. "I told you not to call me that."

Wild Thing sort of pushed Denny away. "Yeah? What are you gonna do about it?"

"You could find out right now, jerk, if you wanted to step outside." Denny took hold of the vest again. "But of course you've got a good excuse. You have to go play your guitar." Denny said "guitar" the way people usually say the word "homework."

"I'll tell you what, Meat. I'll be out there after two songs. Then we'll settle this."

"Oh, great." Pam pushed her way between them. "Just what we need. A fight. What a pair of juveniles."

Denny and Wild Thing were past the point of turning back. Even if a girl they both liked was ticked.

Denny started for the door. Then he turned around. "Don't forget. Two songs. If you're not out there, I'll come up on that stage and get you."

"Don't worry, Meat, I'll be there."

Denny headed for the door again and I caught up with him. "Do you really think this is such a hot idea?"

"It's the only idea, French. That guy is a first-class jerk. It's time to pay him back for ripping off our locker room."

"But Coach Briggs said..."

"Don't bother telling me what Briggs said," Denny said, cutting me off. "I've had it with that long-haired puke."

We walked outside. It was pretty cold out, but not enough to cool off Denny.

"Are you sure this isn't a fight over a girl?" I asked him. "Which is a pretty dumb reas—"

He cut me off again. "It's got nothing to do with Pam. Somebody's got to teach that—"

This time it was Denny who got cut off. And not by me. We'd been standing on the front step of the school. A few other kids were hanging around out there. Some were smoking. A couple were sneaking drinks from beer they had stashed on them.

But that wasn't what stopped Denny—and me—cold. No, it was something a lot more scary.

Two cars pulled up in front of the school, and seven or eight guys jumped out of the cars and started up the stairs. I recognized them. Or at least I recognized their jackets. They were from the Devil's Platoon!

I'd only seen them a couple of times but everybody knew about the Platoon. These were very creepy guys from the other side of the city.

They came straight up the stairs and headed for the door. By the time they got there Mr. White, my English teacher, who was supervising the dance, was waiting for them.

Mr. White's not a big guy. To tell you the truth, I'd always thought he was kind of a wimp. I'll give him credit, though; he stood there like he was a defensive end.

"Sorry, gentlemen," he said. "Nobody gets in without a ticket."

One of the Platoon, a very large dude, stepped up to Mr. White. "We got tickets, man, see?" He held a ticket up to Mr. White's face.

Now I didn't think anybody at school would've sold these guys tickets. Mr. White must have figured the same thing.

"Where did you get this?" he asked the guy as he took the ticket and looked at it.

"We bought 'em, of course. How else would we get them?"

"Well, I'm afraid it doesn't matter," Mr. White said. "This is a closed dance."

"Yeah? That's not what we heard."

"Well, you just heard it now."

"Is that so, Teach?" the Platoon guy said. "And who's gonna stop us from going in there? You?"

That's when Denny got into the act. "Him… and us," he said and walked over and stood right in front of the guy.

There are times when having somebody who's fearless for a best friend really sucks. This was one of those times.

I looked around and noticed that most of the other kids who had been outside had disappeared. Like magic. The only people on the steps of the school were Mr. White, Denny, me, and a whole herd of guys from the Devil's Platoon. The night had taken a definite turn for the worse.

5

I figured between the two of us, Mr. White and I could maybe handle the littlest guy. That meant Denny would only have six or seven of them to take care of.

"Take a hike, Meat."

At first I thought Denny had said it. Like he was imitating Wild Thing or something. But it wasn't Denny at all. It was ol' W.T. himself. He'd come up all quiet and I hadn't even noticed him until he spoke. And for once he wasn't talking to Denny. Instead he was looking at the leader of the Platoon.

He came up and stood next to me. What was really strange was the way he was holding his guitar—sort of like a baseball bat.

I could see the words Fender Stratocaster right there on the neck. I figured we were probably talking about maybe fifteen hundred bucks' worth of guitar. And here was Wild Thing looking like he planned to smack some heads with it.

I guess the Devil's Platoon thought it was a bluff. Because the next thing I knew there was chaos on the steps.

There were quite a few surprises in that fight. The biggest one for me was that I actually lived through it.

The second one was that Mr. White wasn't too bad in a scrap. I don't know if he actually threw any punches, because I was a little too busy to be watching him. But one time I glanced over and he had this one guy's arm twisted behind his back and sort of booted him down the stairs.

"Awright, Mr. White!"

Denny and the leader of the Platoon were about even and they were duking it out pretty good. Me, I was trying to do the bumblebee thing. You know, buzz around, cause a little pain here, a little sting there. I kicked a couple of shins, gave one guy a pretty good elbow to the kidney, and almost broke my hand when I actually punched somebody. I figure that guy had about the hardest head on the planet.

But the difference in the fight was definitely Wild Thing. He wasn't bluffing about the guitar. A Fender Stratocaster makes a very interesting noise when it makes contact with something as empty as a Platoon guy's skull, even if the guitar isn't plugged into an amplifier at the time.

About the time Wild Thing rang the guitar off his third target, the Platoon started to lose interest in fighting. A few final shoves between Denny and the leader, and the gang stumbled back down the stairs and into the cars. I'm not making up the stumbling thing. A couple of them were in rough shape.

Before they drove away, the leader leaned his head out the window. "We'll be seeing you creeps again. All of you." Then he called us a couple of names that don't usually come up in Mr. White's English class. And they drove off.

The four of us just stood there on the steps not saying anything. Mr. White was smiling like crazy. Maybe getting to smack some teenagers around after all those years of teaching English was good for the guy.

It was getting kind of uncomfortable. Somebody needed to say something. "Thanks, W.T.," I said.

Nobody else said a word. Not a word. I elbowed Denny in the ribs.

"Yeah," he said finally. What a speech. No "awright" or "Thanks, Buddy." Just, "yeah."

W.T. was checking his guitar over. I figured the least it would need was tuning.

"Don't worry about it, Meat," Wild Thing told Denny. "I wasn't out here to help you. I just didn't want some losers wreckin' the dance. As far as I'm concerned, you and me still got something to settle."

Mr. White finally stopped smiling and stepped between them. "Not tonight, guys. There's been enough fighting for one dance. Let's get back to some music. And by the way, thanks…all three of you."

Denny and Wild Thing glared at one another for a few more seconds. Then Wild Thing went back inside. Mr. White put one hand on my shoulder and one on Denny's and the three of us went back into the school together.

I looked at the clock. Ten to twelve. Not even midnight and I'd already fallen in love and cleaned up on the Devil's Platoon. Well, okay, maybe that's a slight exaggeration.

But what the heck. Surviving a brawl with the Platoon is almost like cleaning up on them. And, yeah, I have to admit, I did have a little help.

And, of course, the night wasn't over yet. There was still the matter of two guys who didn't like each other, but who both liked Pam Parlee.

I figured there might be a little more excitement before I hit the sack that night.

Actually though, that part of it was fairly boring. Denny and Pam had a few more dances and then Pam left with her girlfriends.

Naturally, Denny the Stud never quite got around to asking her if he could walk her home. At least Pam didn't go to The Heavy Breathers' party, so I figured there might still be hope for Denny.

The dance was kind of winding down. Denny and I were leaning against a wall downing a couple of pops when Mr. White came over.

"Listen, guys, the Devil's Platoon aren't people to mess with," he said. "If they try anything, anything at all, let the police know. Or, let me know and I'll talk to the police."

"Okay, Mr. White," I said and Denny nodded. I knew he was thinking, *Yeah, sure, Mr. White.*

"Hey, Mr. White," I said, "have you still got the ticket that jerk said he bought?"

"I think so," he fished in his pocket. "Uh-huh, right here."

I took a look at it. "Hey, that's my ticket! That's the one I bought that got stolen out of my locker at football practice."

"Are you sure?" Mr. White asked me.

"Yeah," I nodded. "I remember, it was number 28. I figured when I bought it that it would be sort of lucky 'cause the twenty-eighth is my birthday."

"I guess we'll have to start locking the room during practices and games," Mr. White said. "Well, thanks again. I'd have been in a lot of trouble if you hadn't helped."

"No problem," Denny said.

"I don't suppose it would be worth a few bonus marks on our Shakespeare exam next week," I said, grinning. Heck, you can't blame a guy for trying.

Mr. White smiled and patted me on the head and walked away to talk to some other students.

"You know what this means, don't you?" I asked Denny.

"No bonus marks on the exam?" Denny laughed.

"No, I mean the ticket." I shook my head. "If those creeps had the dance tickets it means it was them and not Wild Thing who ripped off our locker room."

"Could be, French," Denny said slowly, "but it doesn't matter. Mr. W.T. Zahara and me are going to have it out one day. And when we do, he's going to need more than a guitar to save his hide."

One more thing happened that night. I live pretty close to school so I walked home after the dance. I'd just turned the corner on the street where I live when I saw a car down the road a way. It looked like one of the cars the Platoon had been driving. I told myself it was just my imagination.

Turns out I was wrong.

6

I'd never had any broken bones before. Weird, huh? Most of my friends had broken an arm or collarbone or something falling out of trees or wrecking their bikes when they were little. But not me. Even though I play hockey and football, I didn't have a clue what it was like to have something broken.

Until that night, that is.

They got me about two houses from home. I saw them coming but they drove the car up on the sidewalk to stop me.

It all happened so fast. Probably only took a few seconds. My dad told me later that he heard me yelling, but by the time he could get outside, it was over.

I tried to run first. Then I tried to fight. There were just too many of them. And anyway, I've already explained that I'm not the greatest fighter around.

I'm not sure exactly what happened. I remember this pain exploding in my face and everything spinning around so fast I felt like the top of my head was coming off. That's when I must've passed out.

I woke up the next day in the hospital. The doctor said I was lucky.

I didn't feel lucky. It was my jaw that had been broken. Plus, some of my teeth were chipped and a couple were missing, there were some stitches inside my mouth, and I had a concussion.

Yeah, real lucky.

I only saw myself in a mirror for a couple of seconds. That was enough. It was pretty gross.

My parents were with me when I woke up. They'd been there the whole time. One of the nurses told me that. I wanted to thank them but my jaw was all wired so I couldn't talk to tell them anything.

Denny was my first visitor. He came after school on Monday. I'd had a lot of painkillers and stuff and I kept falling asleep while he was talking. But every time I woke up, he was still there. And still talking. Which was very weird, since a long sentence for Denny is, "Let's go for some fries."

Of course I couldn't answer him, but when I was awake, I watched him and listened. I noticed that the whole time he was clenching and unclenching his fists. Just before he left, he leaned over the bed close to me.

"I know you can't talk, French," he said, "but all I want you to do is nod your head. If it was the Devil's Platoon who did this to you, just nod." I knew why he was asking. Denny was just dumb enough to take on the Platoon to get even for me. And I knew how that would end up. I didn't need my best friend in the next bed in the hospital.

He asked me three times but I never moved my head. Finally he left.

It wasn't that I couldn't nod my head; I could do that much. But I was afraid. It was as simple as that. And I wasn't just afraid for him. If I told Denny or anybody, I knew they'd get me again. One part of the whole thing that I remembered very clearly was the leader of the Platoon telling me what would happen if I ever told anybody—ever.

And one thing I knew for sure, I'd do any-thing—anything—to make sure nothing like that ever happened to me again. If that made me a coward, that was fine.

So, when the police came the next day, and Mr. White and my parents—when all of them asked me, I wouldn't tell. I couldn't tell.

Eventually I was able to talk again. Although I had to do it like a ventriloquist, without mov-ing my lips.

That's when the pressure got a little more intense to tell who'd done it.

But my story was always the same. It was dark and I couldn't see. I had no idea who they were. Of course, I really did know. I'd seen the leader of the Platoon face to face; he'd made sure of that. There was a look on his face, a sort of hate-grin that I'll never forget.

I'd seen that look, that face, every night since they'd jumped me. It was the one dream I could count on. And the worst part was that I couldn't talk to anybody about it.

Coach Briggs came to see me toward the end of the week. I could talk by then, very softly, but I couldn't smile. So I just looked at him.

"I brought you a milkshake, French." He handed me a root beer shake.

I figured he must've asked Denny what my favourite flavour was.

"Thanks." I took the shake and carefully worked the straw between my lips. I could only take a little bit, but man, did it taste good.

All I'd been eating up to then was this watered-down pudding junk. It tasted like a mixture of toilet bowl cleanser and very old Cream of Wheat.

"I'll be ready for St. Joseph's, Coach," I told him. Except when I talked there were long pauses between the words. So it sounded more like, "I'll…be…ready…"

"Don't worry about that, French." He reached over and patted my arm. "You just heal up real good. There's always next year."

I didn't want next year. I wanted *this* year. Thinking about the St. Joe's game was the only thing that kept me from going totally buggy in the hospital.

"Who's…playing…half…back?" I asked him, although I really didn't want to know. I guess I was hoping he'd say nobody, French, we're saving that spot for you.

But that isn't what he said. What he said was, "We've been using W.T. He's looking pretty good, too."

Then he added, "Of course, he's no French in there."

Yeah, right, Coach, I thought.

When he'd gone I just lay there for a long time staring at the ceiling. W.T. Zahara. Wild Thing as halfback.

That night my dream had two faces in it. First the grinning hate-face. And then Wild

Thing. A big smile on his face right after he scored the winning touchdown against St. Joseph's.

I couldn't get back to sleep after that dream.

7

My first day back at school was interesting, to say the least. I had most of my stitches out, but I hadn't started the dentist stuff yet. That meant that I mumbled through my broken and missing teeth, and, of course, my jaw was still wired. At least the long pauses between words were gone.

I knew I didn't look too great. The lower half of my face and upper half of my neck were purple. Actually, that was an improvement. For the first few days after I got hurt, they were black. Rubber-boot black. And I was swollen, like my whole face had the mumps.

Of course, every kid I saw asked me who did it. I got lots of practice shrugging my shoulders and saying, "Don't know. Didn't see 'em."

After school I went to football practice. I wasn't going to go but I saw Coach Briggs in the hall after math, and he said he wanted me to be an assistant coach for the rest of the season. I didn't want to coach; I wanted to play. But I knew he was trying to be nice, so I figured I should at least show up. It was tough standing on the sidelines watching. It was even tougher seeing Wild Thing play my position. Especially since he played it better than me. Maybe better than any high school halfback I'd ever seen.

Near the end of the practice, I was tossing a ball back and forth with one of the real assistant coaches. Wild Thing came over to me.

"Hi," he said.

"Hi."

"Listen, French, I'm sorry about what happened to you."

"Yeah."

"I'm not trying to take your spot on the team. It's just that they needed somebody in there."

"Forget it. Just make sure you get about four touchdowns against St. Joe's."

He smiled at me. "No problem. You think you'll be able to play?"

"Naw. Probably not."

"Listen, French, I know you're not saying who did it and I don't blame you. But I've got a few friends who can be a little nasty and..."

I shook my head. "Uh-uh, there's been enough of that stuff. Let's leave it alone."

"Okay." He put his hand on my shoulder. "But if you need anything, just yell, all right?"

"I'm not very good at yelling right now," I told him.

"Just whisper then," he smiled. "I mean it, okay?"

"Thanks."

"Sure." He started to walk away, then looked back at me. "See you."

"Listen, W.T., I was wondering..."

"Yeah?" He stopped and turned around.

"Do you...do you really like Pam?"

"Pam?"

"You know, Pam Parlee. The girl at the dance."

"Oh, her."

"See, Denny's kind of liked her for about two years now. I mean, really liked her and..."

"Hey," Wild Thing looked around and then lowered his voice, "let me tell you something. I'm going out with someone right now. No high school girl either. This woman is twenty-two."

"Wow." I would have whistled but I couldn't make my lips do that yet. "But then why were you . . . you know . . . hangin' around her at the dance and stuff?"

Wild Thing laughed then. "Just to bug Meat. And I think it worked. I know he's your friend, but anything I can do to get to that big jerk..."

"He's not a bad guy really," I said.

"Yeah, right. That's why he made me feel so welcome my first day at school. And told everybody I was the one who ripped off the locker room."

"I know," I nodded. "It was pretty stupid. But I wish you guys could, you know, get along or something."

"Hey, don't sweat it, French, all right?" He started to run back out onto the field. "See ya, buddy."

"Yeah," I said quietly. "I'll see ya."

I stopped into the locker room after practice and said hi to some of the guys. I was getting ready to head out when Coach Briggs came in.

He waved at me and I went over to where he was standing.

"How's our newest assistant coach?" He grinned at me.

"Uh...listen, Coach...I know why you told me I could be an assistant coach and everything, and I appreciate it...but I...don't think..."

Coach Briggs nodded. "That's okay, French," he said. "I understand. I just wanted you to know that as far as all of us are concerned, you're still part of this team. And you're welcome to come around anytime."

"Yeah, well, if it's okay...maybe I'll kind of hang out at practices...." I wasn't sure why I wanted to do that. Well, actually I did know. I still had this crazy idea that maybe a miracle would come along and I'd get into the St. Joseph's game. Weird, I know, but when you've had a dream as long as I had that one, it's hard to let go.

I was starting to feel like a geek standing around the locker room with nothing to do so I headed for the door.

As I was going out, I heard Denny call out, "Hey, French, you're our man, don't forget it, okay?"

Then Wild Thing yelled, "Lookin' good, French man."

I kept going. As the door closed behind me, I was thinking, *yeah, right guys*.

I hadn't gone five steps from the locker room when I almost ran right into one person I definitely did not want to see—Annette Difolia. And me with a face like a jack-o'-lantern.

She said hi but I kept on going. Walked right by her.

It sure was great to be back at school.

8

The next day I thought my luck might be starting to change.

English was first period and it was the day of our Shakespeare exam. I hadn't opened a book since the night the Platoon had rearranged my face, and I knew I'd get killed on the test.

Except there wasn't one; it was postponed. In fact, Mr. White wasn't even there. We had a sub.

Actually she seemed kind of nice—Miss George, I think she said her name was. She divided us up into teams and we had a spelling bee.

It was totally fun, even though there were a few kids who were doing the "hassle the sub" routine.

It was my turn. I was supposed to go up to the board and spell "accommodate" but I never got a chance.

There was a knock at the door. Miss George answered it, then she turned to me.

"A couple of people here to see you, Marcel," she said.

I went out into the hall. Two cops were standing there. I recognized one of them. His name was Sergeant McCready. He'd been to the hospital to talk to me a couple of days after I got beaten up.

I figured it was going to be another pitch to get me to tell them who'd done the number on me. I was getting tired of the whole situation.

"Guys, I already told you everything."

"Yeah, so you said," McCready said.

The other one took out a pad of paper. "There's been a new development, Marcel."

"Oh?" I looked at him.

"There was another attack last night. A guy was changing his tire by the side of the road. He got jumped the same way you did."

I looked at the floor. The pain I'd felt when it happened all came back to me. For a minute, I thought I was going to be sick.

"There's a difference this time," the first cop said. "They hurt this guy even worse. If some people hadn't come along when they did, he could have bled to death."

I was still looking at the floor. There was so much to think about. Sure, I wanted those guys to get caught. But what if I spoke out and something happened and they got off? You hear about that stuff happening all the time. And the next time the Platoon got me, I could be the one left to bleed to death.

"Did he see 'em?" I looked at the cops.

"Don't know. He hasn't regained consciousness," McCready told me. "One of the people living on the street saw some guys running away. Described a jacket that sounded a lot like the ones the Devil's Platoon wear." The guy with the pad wrote something down.

The other cop came over and put his hand on my shoulder. He seemed like a pretty good guy, actually. "Marcel, if we don't get these guys, they're going to keep doing this. And maybe somebody's going to get killed. Now we know there was trouble with the Platoon at the dance, and you helped get rid of them.

"If you saw something, anything at all…"

I pulled away from them. "I told you fifty times, I didn't see anything. Now why don't you just leave me alone?"

"Okay, Marcel." McCready handed me a card. "If you change your mind, this is how you can reach us. Oh, there's one more thing…"

"Yeah?"

"Yeah. The guy they hurt last night was your teacher, Mr. White."

The cops turned and walked away. I stood there in the hall for a long time.

Mr. White was hurt. And they'd said it was bad—said he could've died.

I looked at the card McCready had given me. It was a business card with the phone number of the police station on it.

I stared at it for a long time. I was trying to tell myself that I owed it to Mr. White to make that phone call. He'd stood up to those creeps at the dance.

Geez, if an English teacher could do that, then the least I could do was to—

The trouble was, I couldn't forget that night. And just thinking about it made the pain start all over again, just like when it happened.

I looked up and down the hall. The walls were covered with pictures of students who've gone to Lawrence. But when I looked, it seemed like every picture was of that Platoon guy's face. And the look on every one of those faces was exactly how he looked when he was telling me what they'd do to me if I ever told.

And what happened to Mr. White was proof that those guys weren't fooling around.

I didn't feel much like a spelling bee anymore, so I went down the hall until I came to the music room. It was empty so I went inside.

I sat there in the dark for a long time trying to figure out what had happened to my life.

9

The next day didn't start off so hot. Right after she told us she'd be our sub for at least a week, Miss George sprung a surprise, in-class essay on us. We had to write on a topic of importance to all citizens.

I decided to write about violence in the streets. Mr. White is always telling us to write about something we know. I figured I was like a total expert on that particular subject.

After English I was walking to math with Denny. We were talking, and I don't know, maybe we weren't paying attention. Anyway, the twelfth graders were coming around the corner.

Maybe it was an accident, who knows? Maybe Wild Thing had his head down. Whatever it was, Wild Thing and Denny ran into each other. Big-time. Books flew everywhere.

At first I didn't realize what was happening. And before I got it figured out, the two of them were slamming each other against lockers and having it out right there in the hall.

Everybody else backed off to give them room. Pretty soon, the fists were flying and they both got in some pretty good licks.

That's when I lost it. I went charging right in between them. I pushed Denny, then I pushed Wild Thing, then Denny again.

If one of their fists had come in contact with my busted up face, I'd have been back in the hospital in a hurry. I guess I didn't think about that.

Having this peewee-sized guy jumping in there trying to break it up must have surprised them, because both of them quit swinging and just stood there. They were looking at each other and at me.

"What's wrong with you idiots anyway?" I screamed. (Remember, I said I lost it.)

"Take a look at this!" I pointed to my face. "This is what can happen if you keep screwin' around."

I started to walk away but then I decided I had more to say.

"You know something? You guys are just as bad as the Platoon. If you want to fight so bad, there's a lot of creeps you could save it for. Like, how about St. Joseph's for example? I'd give anything in the world for a shot at those guys. And you two stand here smackin' each other around! One of you could get hurt and miss the game. At least think about your teammates, if your dinosaur brains can't figure anything else out."

By then my mouth was killing me. That time I did walk away. As I started down the hall, I could hear some of the kids saying stuff like "Awright, French!" and "You da man."

Of course, I didn't know what Denny and Wild Thing thought of my little tantrum. Denny didn't talk to me or even look at me in math class. To tell the truth, I didn't really care.

I went to football practice again after school, even though it was pretty obvious my dream of playing was dead and buried. I don't know, maybe I figured I might as well watch Wild Thing totally destroy my future as a halfback.

Or maybe it was just to keep my mind off what had happened to Mr. White.

By the end of the day, it was all over the school that he'd been beaten up. And I imagine a lot of people figured that Mr. White had got it from the same guys that jumped me.

I could feel everybody looking at me, and I knew what they were thinking: *Well, now for sure he'll talk to the cops.*

I felt like screaming, "You're wrong! I'm not talking to anybody. I'm not taking a chance on getting myself killed . . . not even for Mr. White. So leave me alone!"

It was a pretty quiet practice—only a week and a half until the St. Joseph's game and nobody was fooling around. It seemed like everybody was bearing down a little harder.

I figured if a Lawrence team was ever going to beat St. Joe's, this might be the team to do it. And I wouldn't be part of it. Terrific.

After practice I was walking out to the parking lot where Mom was waiting to give me a ride home. The practice had been a long one and it was dark.

Wild Thing came running up to me. "Can I talk to you a minute, French?"

"Yeah."

"What you did at school today..."

"Yeah?"

"Well, you were right. I just wanted you to know."

"Yeah...whatever."

"And you're awful gutsy for a tenth grader."

I smiled as much as my face would let me. "Thanks."

"Listen, I've been thinking. Last year we had a guy on the team I played for in Vancouver who broke his cheekbone."

I just looked at him.

"Anyway," he went on, "the team had a special helmet built for him. Protected his face like crazy. He wound up getting back in for our playoff games."

"Really?"

"Yeah, and I figured I'd give my old coach a call and see if he'd courier it out here and you could try it. I kind of went ahead and did it. Anyway it should be here today or maybe tomorrow."

"Wicked!" I said, but I didn't stay excited for long. "What's the use? The doctor and my parents probably wouldn't let me play anyway."

"It wouldn't hurt to try," Wild Thing said.

"Yeah, I guess maybe it wouldn't,"

"Well, now, look what we have here."

I didn't see who had said it but it wasn't long before I knew. The Devil's Platoon guys stepped out from behind a van.

"Oh no," I whispered.

"Don't worry, pup, we're all finished with you." The leader was grinning at me. "As long as you keep your mouth shut. We came to have a little talk with your friend here."

"Run, W.T!" I screamed.

Wild Thing turned but it was too late. They had us surrounded. There was no place to go.

The Platoon grabbed Wild Thing and the

first thing they did was rip his jacket off him. It was a leather jacket. Real nice.

Wild Thing fought like a caged wolf, but he didn't have a chance. Pretty soon they had his arms pinned and they were dragging him over behind a fence. One of them had hold of me too. But it was just to make sure I wouldn't run off or yell or anything.

I was going to have to watch them do to Wild Thing what they'd done to me.

That's when I heard the noise. Engine noise, real loud. A car came across the parking lot like a top fuel dragster. It almost hit me. The guy holding me let go so he could scramble out of the way. I did the same thing.

Then the car gunned it and headed right at the guys holding Wild Thing. They started diving in every direction.

One of them must have panicked and jumped right at the car. He wound up bouncing up and over the hood.

There was more noise then. The squeal of brakes and tires as the car slammed to a stop right in the middle of all the confusion.

"Get in!" the voice inside the car yelled.

Wild Thing and I dove in and the car roared out of there. It fired rocks and gravel all over those guys. I could hear them yelling. Mostly in pain.

But it was the voice of the driver that really shocked me.

"Mom?" I said when I finally got myself straightened up on the seats.

"You guys okay?" she asked.

"Yeah, I think so," I said.

"Yeah, no problem." Wild Thing was looking out the back window at the crazy scene behind us.

"Geez, Mom, I didn't know you could drive like that," I told her.

"Well I don't make a habit of it." My mom looked over at me and smiled.

I couldn't believe it. That was the second time in a week I'd been surprised by adults. First Mr. White at the dance, and now Mom. Maybe there was hope for the older generation after all.

10

I didn't get much sleep that night, so school the next morning was like walking in a weird fog.

Things picked up in a big way right after psychology. I was on my way to English when Annette Difolia came up and told me she was having a party after the St. Joe's game and would I come?

For a second my mouth almost got ahead of my brain and said no. But then I thought about dancing with Annette. I figured since I wasn't going to get to play in the game, the party might be just what I needed.

"You want this face at your party?" I asked her.

She smiled a smile at me that I'd go to war for. "Well, to tell you the truth...um...I was sort of hoping you'd be with me at the party. Sort of ...my date."

For the first time I understood what happened to Denny whenever Pam Parlee showed up. It took me four tries before I could manage to sputter, "Well...yeah...great...uh, great."

"Okay, I'll see you later, French." She smiled again and headed off down the hall.

As I walked into English, I remembered we were starting *Romeo and Juliet* today. Excellent!!

After sixty-five minutes with the Montagues and the Capulets, I had some free time. I wandered toward the twelfth-grade lockers. I guess I was hoping to see W.T. We hadn't really talked much about the close call with the Platoon.

He was leaning against his locker, and when he saw me he waved me over.

"French, my man, have I got something to show you." He reached into his locker.

What he took out looked like a cross between a football helmet and something you'd wear on a mission to Saturn.

"This is it!" He held it up high. "It got here last night. You wear this puppy and a cement truck couldn't hurt your face."

I looked at it, and I had to admit it seemed pretty well bomb-proof.

"Sweet." I took the helmet and turned it over a couple of times. "You really think it'll work?"

"I guarantee it," he said with a grin. "I'll keep it here and take it to practice for you."

"Thanks," I said.

He put the helmet back in his locker and that's when I saw it. At first I thought it must be a toy or something. But it was no toy. On the top shelf of Wild Thing's locker was a knife. Not just a knife—a switchblade knife.

"Wh . . . what's that?" I imagine my mouth was wide open.

He closed his locker fast. "Forget you saw that, French."

"Yeah, but geez—"

"Listen . . ." He put his hand on my shoulder. "If those creeps come around again, I'm not going to just stand there and let them cripple me . . . or kill me."

"I know," I whispered, "but a switchblade. They kick you out of school for having...where'd you get it?"

"I told you to forget it," he said, and then he grinned again. "Start thinking about what you're going to do to St. Joe's."

"Yeah...I guess so." I turned and started for the study hall. I looked back at him. "W.T.—"

"See ya, French." He waved and headed off down the hall.

"Yeah...see ya," I said.

I figure some of the most important stuff that happens in schools happens in the halls. That's what teachers and parents don't understand. They figure the classrooms are where it's all happening.

So far I'd had two major surprises happen to me that day in the tacky, old halls of Lawrence High. And I wasn't finished yet.

Right after lunch, I caught up with Denny. We were on our way to chem class. He looked kind of depressed, but he always looks that way before chem. *After* chem, too, come to think of it.

"What's happenin'?" I asked.

He didn't answer, which isn't like Denny. Even when he's grumpy, he'll usually talk to me.

"Hey, something wrong?" I tried again.

He turned to look at me then. "I heard what happened to you and Wild Thing last night."

"Yeah, we were lucky my mom saved our butts," I told him.

"You know something, French...?"

"What?"

Whatever it was he wanted to say, he was having trouble, I could see that.

"What?" I said again.

He looked down at the floor. "There's one guy who was at the school dance that night that they haven't got to yet."

"Yeah?"

"Yeah...me," Denny didn't look up and he didn't say anything else. He just walked into chemistry class.

But I knew. And it shook me up too. The toughest guy I've ever known was scared. Real scared.

I thought about it all through class. Mr. Brecht was telling us all about how to calculate molecular mass, but I didn't take much of it in.

The way I figured it, Denny was right. It was just a matter of time until they got him alone somewhere, and there'd be enough of them that even Denny wouldn't have a chance.

Then there was Wild Thing. He had his own answer to the problem. But what an answer. And what happens once the shooting starts? Where do you go from there? Jail? The hospital? The morgue?

And what about Mom? One of those creeps might have got the licence number of the car or something. And if they figured out who she was, would they back off because she's a woman? I knew the answer to that question and I hated it.

There was only one person who could stop this. I hated that too. Why couldn't it be somebody else? Anybody else.

11

At football practice, I actually got to suit up. That was because there wasn't any hitting that day— just drills and stuff. The new helmet felt pretty good, although it rubbed in a couple of places.

Right near the end of the practice Coach Briggs told me I could dress for the St. Joe's game and be on the sidelines but that was it. He figured it was still too dangerous, even with the helmet, for me to play.

I wasn't in a terrific mood as I walked home after practice. I had the helmet with me. I figured Dad and I could adjust it so it wouldn't rub. I might as well be comfortable as I watched the biggest football game of my life.

That's when a guy stepped out from behind a van that was parked on the street. I recognized the jacket right away. It was the first time I'd seen a Platoon guy without all the rest of them around.

I'm pretty sure it was just coincidence that he happened along at that moment. I also don't think he was planning to do anything on his own, but I guess he couldn't resist the temptation to heap some verbal abuse on somebody as small as me.

"Hey, Puke," he said.

"Hey, Puke yourself," I answered.

I'm not sure why I said that. Like I mentioned, I was in a bad mood. Or maybe I'd just had enough.

"Oh, the little man thinks he's tough, huh?" He took a step toward me. "I can see I'm going to have to give you another little lesson in respect."

"Without all your goon friends? I doubt it… Meat." I knew right away why Wild Thing called people he didn't like "Meat." It feels kind of good when you say it.

The Platoon guy put his head down. I wish I could say I did something heroic. But I didn't. I saw him coming, so I held the helmet out in front of me for protection. That's all.

And Platoon loser-guy hit it. Hit it hard. There was a neat sort of "thunk" sound when he ran his head up against that helmet. Almost as neat as the sound Wild Thing's Fender Stratocaster made the night of the dance.

Actually there were two "thunks." The first one was the dork hitting the helmet. The second one was when he crumpled onto the sidewalk. He lay there whining and sniveling like a little kid who's dropped his ice cream cone.

I stepped over him like Clint Eastwood in a western movie and started down the street. But I didn't go far.

There was a little grocery store on the corner. I stepped into the doorway and pulled out my cell phone and the card I'd been given. I dialed the number and when a voice came on the line, I said, "Hello, this is Marcel Boileau. I'd like to speak to Sergeant McCready, please."

12

The morning of the St. Joe's game, I had to go to the police station to make a statement.

I was still kind of nervous about the idea of testifying in court against the Platoon. But in a way I was relieved to have made the decision.

When we were finished, Sergeant McCready gave me a ride to the stadium. I was the only player who got a police escort to the game that day.

I put on my equipment just like I was going to play. Except I wasn't. Coach Briggs and my parents had had a meeting and agreed I could injure myself again, helmet or no helmet. So I'd be on the sidelines watching the rest of the guys. Drag.

I tried not to let on that it was killing me to have to watch. I slapped all the guys on the shoulder pads and gave 'em a lot of rah-rah stuff.

Before the game Coach Briggs told us that the key to St. Joseph's was a guy named Mike Claridge. He was the quarterback and when they were in trouble they put him in on defence, too.

Then Coach diagrammed out a new play on the board. Something called a Naked Sweep Right. All the blockers go left and Carter Kent hands the ball off to Wild Thing who goes around the right side.

It's called a naked sweep because he's out there by himself. The idea is that the defence will go with the blockers and we totally fool 'em.

Then Coach Briggs gave us a little pep talk and we all ran out on the field screaming and yelling like crazy.

I looked over at the St. Joe's bench and saw forty of the biggest guys I've ever seen. Their cheerleaders were bigger than I am.

"No sweat, French," Denny said to me as we were warming up. "Big doesn't necessarily mean tough."

Yeah, right, I thought to myself.

It didn't take long to blow Denny's theory to bits. At the end of the first quarter he came over to me. There was blood and dirt and sweat all over his jersey, and he was puffing like my dad after he goes for his nightly run.

"Those are ... the ... toughest guys I ever ... saw," he gasped.

I just nodded at him. We were hanging in there, though. So far it was nothing—nothing. Our defence was playing great.

In the second quarter, Carter Kent threw a little pass to Wild Thing. But before he could get going, Claridge hit him about as hard as I've ever seen somebody hit somebody. I heard the crunch from across the field.

Wild Thing had to come out of the game for a few minutes while our trainer tried to get his body back in its normal shape.

Coach Briggs put in a kid who didn't play much. Third play in there, the guy fumbled the ball. Five plays later Claridge ran it in and it was St. Joe's 7—Lawrence 0.

And my uniform was still perfectly clean.

In the third quarter, Wild Thing was back in the game. He put on quite a show and we finally got on the scoreboard. It was 7–7.

In the fourth quarter Claridge hit Wild Thing again. Maybe harder than the first time. W.T. didn't want to come out that time but Coach made him sit down for a couple of plays.

On the next play, Denny ran over Claridge like a tank rolling over the Pillsbury Dough Boy. Wild Thing yelled "Awright! Nice hit, Meat!"

Denny turned and looked at our bench and nodded to Wild Thing. It was the first time they'd ever looked at each other without a whole bunch of hate in their eyes.

It didn't help as far as the game went, though. St. Joe's kicked a couple of field goals and they were leading 13–7 with a couple of minutes to play.

We got the ball back with 1:42 showing on the clock. We were on our 30-yard line. Wild Thing made a couple of great runs and Carter

Kent completed a couple of passes and we were on St. Joseph's 27. There was just one small problem. There were twelve seconds left in the game.

Coach Briggs called a time out. He got all the offence together on the sidelines. I was just standing back watching. I didn't figure they needed me in the meeting.

"French, get over here." Coach waved me over.

I walked to where they were huddled up. I figured he just wanted me there to show the togetherness bit.

"Okay, here's the deal," Coach Briggs was saying. "French, you're going in as halfback and Wild Thing, you move to wide receiver."

Now I knew what he was up to. He wanted Carter to throw a long pass to Wild Thing. Not a bad idea.

Boy, was I wrong.

"French, you know how the Naked Sweep Right works?" Coach was talking to me. To me!

"Uh...yeah," I said.

"Well, then grab that wonder helmet of yours and get us a touchdown. I figure they'll put

Claridge on W.T." Coach turned to Wild Thing, "And I want you to line up to the left and run out there and keep him away from the play. Got it?"

Wild Thing nodded and grinned. I put my helmet on but the whole situation was feeling really strange.

"What about my parents? I thought…"

Coach Briggs had moved away to explain something to the "O" line, so I didn't get an answer. I looked up in the bleachers and spotted my dad. He gave me the thumbs-up sign. I couldn't believe it. Sometimes it's hard to figure adults.

I felt like a rookie going in for my first play in my first game. I kept thinking, what if it doesn't work? What if they don't fall for it? And I get in for one play and cost our team the championship.

For a second I actually thought about going back to Coach Briggs and telling him I couldn't do it. That my head was hurting or something stupid like that.

But there was no time. The time out was over and we ran out on the field. As we got into the huddle, a couple of the St. Joe's guys yelled stuff at me. I heard one of them. "Awright. A new puppy to squash. Come and get it, 36."

Since 36 is my number, there wasn't too much doubt about who he was talking to. I tried to concentrate on what Carter Kent was saying.

"OK, Naked Sweep Right. W.T. you split out wide left. This is it, guys. Ready…BREAK."

We ran out over the ball. My hands were sweating so bad, I figured I'd be sure to fumble as soon as Carter handed the ball to me.

I looked out to the left. Wild Thing was lined up about a half mile away. Claridge was with him. So far, so good.

Carter called the signals, the ball was snapped. I held for a two count like I was supposed to and started right.

Carter stuffed the ball into my gut and I ran harder than I've ever run in my life. I got outside and looked toward the end zone.

There was nothing but daylight. Yes! If I didn't fall down, I could run it in and be a hero. And the Lawrence Cowboys would finally be the champs.

That's when I noticed a blur coming at me from the left. I looked that way. For a second I wanted to just stop right there and throw up.

Claridge had figured it out. And he was coming toward me like a runaway logging truck.

It was going to be close. I figured he'd get to me around the five. Then it would just be a question of whether I could carry him into the end zone or not. Not likely.

I crossed the 10 in full flight and braced myself for the hit.

The collision, when it happened, was like an explosion. I'd say 8.5 on the Richter scale. They probably heard it in Tokyo. Two bodies, both running at top speed hitting each other as hard as it's possible to hit.

Only thing is—my body wasn't one of them. That's because W.T., as in Wild Thing Zahara— long-haired, sandal-wearing singer and lead guitar player for the Heavy Breathers—arrived about one millisecond before St. Joseph's star player took my head off.

The crash occurred when Wild Thing left his

feet and threw his body at Claridge. It was the greatest block of all time. No kidding. They landed in a heap on the five yard line and I jogged into the end zone.

Carter Kent kicked the convert, and for the first time in the history of the world the Lawrence High Cowboys had beaten St. Joseph's.

The funny thing is—I still felt like I was in a scene from one of those Italian movies. You know, the ones nobody can ever figure out.

It really felt that way when the final gun sounded and I got mobbed by all the guys on the team. It was the closest I came to getting hurt in the whole deal.

The only two people who weren't hugging me were Wild Thing and Denny. That's because they were too busy hugging each other and high-fiving like crazy.

When I finally got free, I looked over at the bleachers again. My mom and dad were hugging like a couple of teenagers. They waved at me and I waved back.

Then I looked for Annette. She was standing there smiling and waving and mouthing the word "Par-ty".

I grinned back at her, and for the first time in almost a month, my face didn't hurt.